GREAT GHOST STORIES

Troll

This edition published in 2002.

This unabridged edition has been set in a size and style designed for easy reading. Format, type, composition, and design of this book are the exclusive property of Troll Communications L.L.C.

ISBN 0-8167-0468-6

Printed in the United States of America.

10 9 8 7 6 5

Contents

Algernon Blackwood

Keeping His Promise

It was eleven o'clock at night, and young Marriott was locked into his room, cramming as hard as he could cram. He was a "Fourth Year Man" at Edinburgh University and he had been plowed for this particular examination so often that his parents had positively declared they could no longer supply the funds to keep him there.

His rooms were cheap and dingy, but it was the lecture fees that took the money. So Marriott pulled himself together at last and definitely made up his mind that he would pass or die in the attempt, and for some weeks now he had been reading as hard as mortal man can read. He was trying to make up for lost time and money in a way that showed conclusively he did not understand the value of either. For no ordinary man—and Marriott was in every sense an ordinary man—can afford to drive the mind as he had lately been driving his, without sooner or later paying the cost.

Among the students he had few friends or acquaintances, and these few had promised not to disturb him at night, knowing he was at last reading in earnest. It was, therefore, with feelings a good deal stronger than mere surprise that he heard his doorbell ring on this particular night and realized that he was to have a visitor. Some men would simply have muffled the bell and gone on quietly with their work. But Marriott was not this sort. He was nervous. It would have bothered and pecked at his mind all night long not to know who the visitor was and what he wanted. The only thing to do, therefore, was to let him in—and out again—as quickly as possible.

The landlady went to bed at ten o'clock punctually, after which hour nothing would induce her to pretend she heard the bell, so Marriott jumped up from his books with an exclamation that augured ill for the reception of his caller, and prepared to let him in with his own hand.

The streets of Edinburgh town were very still at this late hour—it was late for Edinburgh—and in the quiet neighborhood of F— Street, where Marriott lived on the third floor, scarcely a sound broke the silence. As he crossed the floor, the bell rang a second time, with unnecessary clamor, and he unlocked the door and passed into the little hallway with considerable wrath and annoyance in his heart at the insolence of the double interruption.

"The fellows all know I'm reading for this exam. Why in the world do they come to bother me at such an unearthly hour?"

The inhabitants of the building, with himself, were medical students, general students, poor Writers to the Signet, and some others whose vocations were perhaps not so obvious. The stone staircase, dimly lighted at each floor by a gas jet that would not turn above a certain height, wound down to the level of the street with no pretense at carpet or railing. At some levels it was cleaner than at others. It depended on the landlady of the particular level.

The acoustic properties of a spiral staircase seem to be peculiar. Marriott, standing by the open door, book in hand, thought every moment the owner of the footsteps would come into view. The sound of the boots was so close and so loud that they seemed to travel disproportionately in advance of their cause. Wondering who it would be, he stood ready with all manner of sharp greetings for the man who dared thus to disturb his work. But the man did not appear. The steps sounded almost under his nose, yet no one was visible.

A sudden queer sensation of fear passed over him—a faintness and a shiver down the back. It went, however, almost as soon as it came, and he was just debating whether he would call aloud to his invisible visitor, or slam the door and return to his books, when the cause of the disturbance turned the corner very slowly and came into view.

It was a stranger. He saw a youngish man short of figure and very broad. His face was the color of a piece of chalk and the eyes, which were very bright, had heavy lines underneath them.

Though the cheeks and chin were unshaven and the general appearance unkempt, the man was evidently a gentleman, for he was well dressed and bore himself with a certain air. But, strangest of all, he wore no hat, and carried none in his hand; and although rain had been falling steadily all the evening, he appeared to have neither overcoat nor umbrella.

A hundred questions sprang up in Marriott's mind and rushed to his lips, chief among which was something like "Who in the world are you?" and "What in the name of heaven do you come to me for?" But none of these questions found time to express themselves in words, for almost at once the caller turned his head a little so that the gas light in the hall fell upon his features from a new angle. Then in a flash Marriott recognized him.

"Field! Man alive! Is it you?" he gasped.

The Fourth Year Man was not lacking in intuition, and he perceived at once that here was a case for delicate treatment. He divined, without any actual process of thought, that the catastrophe often predicted had come at last, and that this man's father had turned him out of the house. They had been at a private school together years before, and though they had hardly met once since, the news had not failed to reach him from time to time with considerable detail, for the family lived near his own and between certain of the sisters there was great intimacy. Young Field had gone wild later, he remembered hearing about it all—drink, a woman, opium, or something of the sort—he could not exactly call to mind.

"Come in," he said at once, his anger vanishing. "There's been something wrong, I can see. Come in, and tell me all about it and perhaps I can help——" He hardly knew what to say, and stammered a lot more besides. The dark side of life, and the horror of it, belonged to a world that lay remote from his own select little atmosphere of books and dreamings. But he had a man's heart for all that.

He led the way across the hall, shutting the front door carefully behind him, and noticed as he did so that the other, though certainly sober, was unsteady on his legs, and evidently much exhausted. Marriott might not be able to pass his examinations, but he at least knew the symptoms of starvation—acute starvation, unless he was much mistaken—when they stared him in the face.

"Come along," he said cheerfully, and with genuine sympathy in his voice. "I'm glad to see you. I was going to have a bite of something to eat, and you're just in time to join me."

The other made no audible reply, and shuffled so feebly with his feet that Marriott took his arm by way of support. He noticed for the first time that the clothes hung on him with pitiful looseness. The broad frame was literally hardly more than a frame. He was as thin as a skeleton. But, as he touched him, the sensation of faintness and dread returned. It only lasted a moment, and then passed off, and he ascribed it not unnaturally to the distress and shock of seeing a former friend in such a pitiful plight.

"Better let me guide you. It's shamefully

dark—this hall. I'm always complaining,'' he said lightly, recognizing by the weight upon his arm that the guidance was sorely needed, ''but the old cat never does anything except promise.'' He led him to the sofa, wondering all the time where he had come from and how he had found out the address. It must be at least seven years since those days at the private school when they used to be such close friends.

''Now, if you'll forgive me for a minute,'' he said, ''I'll get supper ready—such as it is. And don't bother to talk. Just take it easy on the sofa. I see you're dead tired. You can tell me about it afterwards, and we'll make plans.''

The other sat down on the edge of the sofa and stared in silence, while Marriott got out the brown loaf, scones, and huge pot of marmalade that Edinburgh students always keep in their cupboards. His eyes shone with a brightness that suggested drugs, Marriott thought, stealing a glance at him from behind the cupboard door. He did not like yet to take a full square look. The fellow was in a bad way, and it would have been so like an examination to stare and wait for explanation. Besides he was evidently almost too exhausted to speak. So, for reasons of delicacy—and for another reason as well which he could not exactly formulate to himself—he let his visitor rest apparently unnoticed, while he busied himself with the supper. He lit the spirit lamp to make cocoa, and when the water was boiling he drew up the table with the good things to the sofa, so that Field need not have even the trouble of moving to a chair.

"Now, let's tuck in," he said, "and afterwards we'll have a pipe and a chat. I'm reading for an exam, you know, and I always have something about this time. It's jolly to have a companion."

He looked up and caught his guest's eyes directed straight upon his own. An involuntary shudder ran through him from head to foot. The face opposite him was deadly white and wore a dreadful expression of pain and mental suffering.

"By Gad!" he said, jumping up, "I quite forgot. I've got some whiskey somewhere. What a fool I am. I never touch it myself when I'm working like this."

He went to the cupboard and poured out a stiff glass which the other swallowed at a single gulp and without any water. Marriott watched him while he drank it, and at the same time noticed something else as well—Field's coat was all over dust, and on one shoulder was a bit of cobweb. It was perfectly dry; Field arrived on a soaking wet night without hat, umbrella, or overcoat, and yet perfectly dry, even dusty. Therefore he had been under cover. What did it all mean? Had he been hiding in the building...?

It was very strange. Yet he volunteered nothing; and Marriott had pretty well made up his mind by this time that he would not ask any questions until he had eaten and slept. Food and sleep were obviously what the poor devil needed most and first—he was pleased with his powers of ready diagnosis—and it would not be fair to press him till he had recovered a bit.

They ate their supper together while the host carried on a running one-sided conversation, chiefly about himself and his exams and his "old cat" of a landlady, so that the guest need not utter a single word unless he really wished to —which he evidently did not! But, while he toyed with his food, feeling no desire to eat, the other ate voraciously. To see a hungry man devour cold scones, stale oatcake, and brown bread laden with marmalade was a revelation to this inexperienced student who had never known what it was to be without at least three meals a day. He watched in spite of himself, wondering why the fellow did not choke in the process.

But Field seemed to be as sleepy as he was hungry. More than once his head dropped and he ceased to masticate the food in his mouth. Marriott had positively to shake him before he would go on with his meal. A stronger emotion will overcome a weaker, but this struggle between the sting of real hunger and the magical opiate of overpowering sleep was a curious sight to the student, who watched it with mingled astonishment and alarm. He had heard of the pleasure it was to feed hungry men, and watch them eat, but he had never actually witnessed it and he had no idea it was like this. Field ate like an animal—gobbled, stuffed, gorged. Marriott forgot his reading, and began to feel somthing very much like a lump in his throat.

"Afraid there's been awfully little to offer you, old man," he managed to blurt out when at length the last scone had disappeared, and the rapid, one-sided meal was at an end. Field still made no reply, for he was almost asleep in his seat. He merely looked up wearily and gratefully.

"Now you must have some sleep, you know," he continued, "or you'll go to pieces. I shall be up all night reading for this blessed exam. You're more than welcome to my bed. Tomorrow we'll have a late breakfast and—and see what can be done—and make plans—I'm awfully good at making plans, you know," he added with an attempt at lightness.

Field maintained his "dead sleepy" silence, but appeared to acquiesce, and the other led the way into the bedroom, apologizing as he did so to this half-starved son of a baronet—whose own home was almost a palace—for the size of the room. The weary guest, however, made no pretence of thanks or politeness. He merely steadied himself on his friend's arm as he staggered across the room, and then, with all his clothes on, dropped his exhausted body on the bed. In less than a minute he was to all appearances sound asleep.

For several minutes Marriott stood in the open door and watched him; praying devoutly that he might never find himself in a like predicament, and then fell to wondering what he would do with his unbidden guest on the morrow. But he did not stop long to think, for the call of his books was imperative, and happen what might, he must see to it that he passed that examination.

Having again locked the door into the hall, he sat down to his books and resumed his notes on *materia medica* where he had left off when the bell rang. But it was difficult for some time to concentrate his mind on the subject. His thoughts kept wandering to the picture of that white-faced, strange-eyed fellow, starved and dirty, lying in his clothes and boots on the bed. He recalled their schooldays together before they had drifted apart, and how they had vowed eternal friendship—and all the rest of it. And now! What horrible straits to be in. How could any man let the love of dissipation take such hold upon him?

But one of their vows together Marriott, it seemed, had completely forgotten. Just now, at any rate, it lay too far in the background of his memory to be recalled.

Through the half-open door—the bedroom led out of the sitting room and had no other door—came the sound of deep, long-drawn breathing, the regular, steady breathing of a tired man, so tired that, even to listen to it made Marriott almost want to go to sleep himself.

"He needed it," reflected the student, "and perhaps it came only just in time!"

Perhaps so; for outside the bitter wind from across the Forth howled cruelly and drove the rain in cold streams against the window panes, and down the deserted streets. Long before Marriott settled down again properly to his reading, he heard distantly, as it were, through the sentences of the book, the heavy, deep breathing of the sleeper in the next room.

A couple of hours later, when he yawned and changed his books, he still heard the breathing, and went cautiously up to the door to look round.

At first the darkness of the room must have deceived him, or else his eyes were confused and dazzled by the recent glare of the reading lamp. For a minute or two he could make out nothing at all but dark lumps of furniture, the mass of the chest of drawers by the wall, and the white patch where his bath stood in the center of the floor.

Then the bed came slowly into view. And on it he saw the outline of the sleeping body gradually take shape before his eyes, growing up strangely into the darkness, till it stood out in marked relief—the long black form against the white counterpane.

He could hardly help smiling. Field had not moved an inch. He watched him a moment or two and then returned to his books. The night was full of the singing voices of the wind and rain. There was no sound of traffic; no hansoms clattered over the cobbles, and it was still too early for the milk carts. He worked on steadily and conscientiously, only stopping now and again to change a book, or to sip some of the poisonous stuff that kept him awake and made his brain so active, and on these occasions Field's breathing was always distinctly audible in the room. Outside, the storm continued to howl, but inside the house all was stillness. The shade of the reading lamp threw all the light upon the littered table, leaving the other end of the room in comparative darkness. The bedroom door was exactly opposite him where he sat. There was nothing to disturb the worker, nothing but an occasional rush of wind against the windows, and a slight pain in his arm.

This pain, however, which he was unable to account for, grew once or twice very acute. It bothered him; and he tried to remember how, and when, he could have bruised himself so severely, but without success.

At length the page before him turned from yellow to gray, and there were sounds of wheels in the street below. It was four o'clock. Marriott leaned back and yawned prodigiously. Then he drew back the curtains. The storm had subsided and the Castle Rock was shrouded in mist. With another yawn he turned away from the dreary outlook and prepared to sleep the remaining four hours till breakfast on the sofa. Field was still breathing heavily in the next room, and he first tiptoed across the floor to take another look at him.

Peering cautiously round the half-opened door his first glance fell upon the bed now plainly discernible in the gray light of morning. He stared hard. Then he rubbed his eyes. Then he rubbed his eyes again and thrust his head farther round the edge of the door. With fixed eyes he stared harder still, and harder.

But it made no difference at all. He was staring into an empty room.

The sensation of fear he had felt when Field first appeared upon the scene returned suddenly, but with much greater force. He became conscious, too, that his left arm was throbbing violently and causing him great pain. He stood wondering, and staring, and trying to collect his thoughts. He was trembling from head to foot.

By a great effort of the will he left the support of the door and walked forward boldly into the room.

There, upon the bed, was the impress of a body, where Field had lain and slept. There was the mark of the head on the pillow, and the slight indentation at the foot of the bed where the boots had rested on the counterpane. And there, plainer than ever—for he was closer to it—was *the breathing!*

Marriott tried to pull himself together. With a great effort he found his voice and called his friend aloud by name!

"Field! Is that you? Where are you?"

There was no reply; but the breathing continued without interruption, coming directly from the bed. His voice had such an unfamiliar sound that Marriott did not care to repeat his questions, but he went down on his knees and examined the bed above and below, pulling the mattress off finally, and taking the coverings away separately one by one. But though the sounds continued there was no visible sign of Field, nor was there any space in which a human being, however small, could have concealed itself. He pulled the bed out from the wall, but the sound *stayed where it was.* It did not move with the bed.

Marriott, finding self-control a little difficult in his weary condition, at once set about a thorough search of the room. He went through the cupboard, the chest of drawers, the little alcove where the clothes hung—everything. But there was no sign of anyone. The small window near the ceiling was closed; and, anyhow, was not large enough to let a cat pass. The sitting-room door was locked on the inside; he could not have got out that way. Curious thoughts began to trouble Marriott's mind, bringing in their train unwelcome sensations. He grew more and more excited; he searched the bed again till it resembled the scene of a pillow fight; he searched both rooms, knowing all the time it was useless—and then he searched again. A cold perspiration broke out all over his body; and the sound of heavy breathing, all this time, never ceased to come from the corner where Field had lain down to sleep.

Then he tried something else. He pushed the bed back exactly into its original position—and himself lay down upon it just where his guest had lain. But the same instant he sprang up again in a single bound. The breathing was close beside him, almost on his cheek, and between him and the wall! Not even a child could have squeezed into the space.

He went back into his sitting room, opened the windows, welcoming all the light and air possible, and tried to think the whole matter over quietly and clearly. Men who read too hard, and slept too little, he knew were sometimes troubled with very vivid hallucinations. Again he calmly reviewed every incident of the night; his accurate sensations; the vivid details; the emotions stirred in him; the dreadful feast—no single hallucination could ever combine all these and cover so long a period of time. But with less satisfaction he thought of the recurring faintness, and curious sense of horror that had once or twice come over him, and then of the violent pains in his arm. These are quite unaccountable.

Moreover, now that he began to analyze and examine, there was one other thing that fell upon him like a sudden revelation: *During the whole time Field had not actually uttered a single word!* Yet, as though in mockery upon his reflections, there came ever from that inner room the sound of the breathing, long-drawn, deep, and regular. The thing was incredible. It was absurd.

Haunted by visions of brain fever and insanity, Marriott put on his cap and mackintosh and left the house. The morning air on Arthur's Seat would blow the cobwebs from his brain; the scent of the heather, and above all, the sight of the sea. He roamed over the wet slopes above Holyrood for a couple of hours, and did not return until the exercise had shaken some of the horror out of his bones, and given him a ravening appetite into the bargain.

As he entered he saw that there was another man in the room, standing against the window with his back to the light. He recognized his fellow student Greene, who was reading for the same examination.

"Read hard all night, Marriott," he said, "and thought I'd drop in here to compare notes and have some breakfast. You're out early?" he added, by way of a question. Marriott said he had a headache and a walk had helped it, and Greene nodded and said "Ah!" But when the girl had set the steaming porridge on the table and gone out again, he went on with rather a forced tone, "Didn't know you had any friends who drank, Marriott?"

This was obviously tentative, and Marriott replied drily that he did not know it either.

"Sounds just as if some chap were 'sleeping it off' in there, doesn't it, though?" persisted the other, with a nod in the direction of the bedroom, and looking curiously at his friend. The two men stared steadily at each other for several seconds, and then Marriott said earnestly—

"Then you hear it too, thank God!"

"Of course I hear it. The door's open. Sorry if I wasn't meant to."

"Oh, I don't mean that," said Marriott, lowering his voice. "But I'm awfully relieved. Let me explain. Of course, if you hear it too, then it's all right; but really it frightened me more than I can tell you. I thought I was going to have brain fever, or something, and you know what a lot depends on this exam. It always begins with sounds, or visions, or some sort of beastly hallucination, and I——"

"Rot!" ejaculated the other impatiently. "What *are* you talking about?"

"Now listen to me, Greene," said Marriott, as calmly as he could, for the breathing was still plainly audible, "and I'll tell you what I mean, only don't interrupt." And thereupon he related exactly what had happened during the night, telling everything, even down to the pain in his arm. When it was over he got up from the table and crossed the room.

"You hear the breathing now plainly, don't you?" he said. Greene said he did. "Well, come with me, and we'll search the room together." The other, however, did not move from his chair.

"I've been in already," he said sheepishly; "I heard the sounds and thought it was you. The door was ajar—so I went in."

Marriott made no comment, but pushed the door open as wide as it would go. As it opened, the sound of breathing grew more and more distinct.

"*Someone* must be in there," said Greene under his breath.

"*Someone* is in there, but *where?*" said Marriott. Again he urged his friend to go in with him. But Greene refused pointblank: said he had been in once and had searched the room and there was nothing there. He would not go in again for a good deal.

They shut the door and retired into the other room to talk it all over with many pipes. Greene questioned his friend very closely, but without illuminating result, since questions cannot alter facts.

"The only thing that ought to have a proper, a logical, explanation is the pain in my arm," said Marriott, rubbing that member with an attempt at a smile. "It hurts so infernally and aches all the way up. I can't remember bruising it, though."

"Let me examine it for you," said Greene. "I'm awfully good at bones in spite of the examiners' opinion to the contrary." It was a relief to play the fool a bit, and Marriott took his coat off and rolled up his sleeve.

"By George, though, I'm bleeding!" he exclaimed. "Look here! What on earth's this?"

On the forearm, quite close to the wrist, was a

thin red line. There was a tiny drop of apparently fresh blood on it. Greene came over and looked closely at it for some minutes. Then he sat back in his chair, looking curiously at his friend's face.

"You've scratched youself without knowing it," he said presently.

"There's no sign of a bruise. It must be something else that made the arm ache."

Marriott sat very still, staring silently at his arm as though the solution of the whole mystery lay there actually written upon the skin.

"What's the matter? I see nothing very strange about a scratch," said Greene, in an unconvincing sort of voice. "It was your cuff links probably. Last night in your excitement——"

But Marriott, white to the very lips, was trying to speak. The sweat stood in great beads on his forehead. At last he leaned forward close to his friend's face.

"Look," he said, in a low voice that shook a little. "Do you see that red mark? I mean *underneath* what you call the scratch?"

Greene admitted he saw something or other, and Marriott wiped the place clean with his handkerchief and told him to look again more closely.

"Yes, I see," returned the other, lifting his head after a moment's careful inspection. "It looks like an old scar."

"It *is* an old scar," whispered Marriott, his lips trembling. "*Now* it all comes back to me."

"All what?" Greene fidgeted on his chair. He tried to laugh, but without success. His friend seemed bordering on collapse.

"Hush! Be quiet, and—I'll tell you," he said. "*Field made that scar.*"

For a whole minute the two men looked each other full in the face without speaking.

"Field made that scar!" repeated Marriott at length in a louder voice.

"Field! You mean—last night?'

"No, not last night. Years ago—at school, with his knife. And I made a scar in his arm with mine." Marriott was talking rapidly now.

"We exchanged drops of blood in each other's cuts. He put a drop into my arm and I put one into his—"

"In the name of heaven, what for?"

"It was a boys' compact. We made a sacred pledge, a bargain. I remember it all perfectly now. We had been reading some dreadful book and we swore to appear to one another—I mean, whoever died first swore to show himself to the other. And we sealed the compact with each other's blood. I remember it all so well—the hot summer afternoon in the playground, seven years ago—and one of the masters caught us and confiscated the knives—and I have never thought of it again to this day—"

"And you mean—" stammered Greene.

But Marriott made no answer. He got up and crossed the room and lay down wearily upon the sofa, hiding his face in his hands.

Greene himself was a bit nonplussed. He left his friend alone for a little while, thinking it all over again. Suddenly an idea seemed to strike him. He went over to where Marriott still lay motionless on the sofa and roused him. In any case it was better to face the matter, whether there was an explanation or not. Giving in was always the silly exit.

"I say, Marriott," he began, as the other turned his white face up to him. "There's no good being so upset about it. I mean—if it's all an hallucination we know what to do. And if it isn't—well, we know what to think, don't we?"

"I suppose so. But it frightens me horribly for some reason," returned his friend in a hushed voice. "And that poor devil—"

"But, after all, if the worst is true and—and that chap *has* kept his promise—well, he has, that's all, isn't it?"

Marriott nodded.

"There's only one thing that occurs to me," Greene went on, "and that is, are you quite sure that—that he really ate like that—I mean that he actually *ate anything at all*?" he finished, blurting out all his thought.

Marriott stared at him for a moment and then said he could easily make certain. He spoke quietly. After the main shock no lesser surprise could affect him.

"I put the things away myself," he said, "after we had finished. They are on the third shelf in that cupboard. No one touched 'em since."

He pointed without getting up, and Greene took the hint and went over to look.

"Exactly," he said, after a brief examination; "just as I thought. It was partly hallucination, at any rate. The things haven't been touched. Come and see for yourself."

Together they examined the shelf. There was the brown loaf, the plate of stale scones, the oatcake all untouched. Even the glass of whiskey Marriott had poured out stood there with the whiskey still in it.

"You were feeding—no one," said Greene. "Field ate and drank nothing. He was not there at all!"

"But the breathing?" urged the other in a low voice, staring with a dazed expression on his face.

Greene did not answer. He walked over to the bedroom, while Marriott followed him with his eyes. He opened the door, and listened. There was no need for words. The sound of deep, regular breathing came floating through the air. There was no hallucination about that, at any rate. Marriott could hear it where he stood on the other side of the room.

Greene closed the door and came back. "There's only one thing to do," he declared with decision. "Write home and find out about him, and meanwhile come and finish your reading in my rooms. I've got an extra bed."

"Agreed," returned the Fourth Year Man; "there's no hallucination about that exam; I must pass that whatever happens."

And this was what they did.

It was about a week later than Marriott got the answer from his sister. Part of it he read out to Greene—

"It is curious," she wrote, "that in your letter you should have inquired after Field. It seems a terrible thing, but you know only a short while ago Sir John's patience became exhausted, and he turned him out of the house, they say without a penny. Well, what do you think? He has killed himself. At least, it looks like suicide. Instead of leaving the house, he went down into the cellar and simply starved himself to death....They're trying to suppress it, of course, but I heard it all from my maid, who got it from their footman....They found the body on the 14th and the doctor said he had died about twelve hours before....He was dreadfully thin....."

"Then he died on the 13th," said Greene.

Marriott nodded.

"That's the very night he came to see you."

Marriott nodded again.

E.F. Benson

Caterpillars

I saw a month ago in an Italian paper that the Villa Casana, in which I once stayed, had been pulled down, and that a manufactory of some sort was in process of erection on its site. There is therefore no longer any reason for refraining from writing of those things which I myself saw (or imagined I saw) in a certain room and on a certain landing of the villa in question, nor from mentioning the circumstances which followed, which may or may not (according to the opinion of the reader) throw some light on, or be somehow connected with this experience.

The Villa Casana was in all ways but one a perfectly delightful house, yet, if it were standing now, nothing in the world—I use the phrase in its literal sense—would induce me to set foot in it again, for I believe it to have been haunted in a very terrible and practical manner. Most ghosts, when all is said and done, do not do much harm;

they may perhaps terrify, but the person whom they visit usually gets over their visitation. They may on the other hand be entirely friendly and beneficent. But the appearances in the Villa Casana were not beneficent, and had they made their "visit" in a very slightly different manner, I do not suppose I should have got over it any more than Arthur Inglis did.

The house stood on an ilex-clad hill not far from Sestri di Levante on the Italian Riviera, looking out over the iridescent blues of that enchanted sea, while behind it rose the pale green chestnut woods that climb up the hillsides till they give place to the pines that, black in contrast with them, crown the slopes. All round it the garden in the luxuriance of mid-spring bloomed and was fragrant, and the scent of magnolia and rose, borne on the salt freshness of the winds from the sea, flowed like a stream through the cool, vaulted rooms.

On the ground floor a broad pillared *loggia* ran round three sides of the house, the top of which formed a balcony for certain rooms on the first floor. The main staircase, broad and of gray marble steps, led up from the hall to a landing outside these rooms, which were three in number, namely, two big sitting rooms and a bedroom arranged *en suite*. The latter was unoccupied, the sitting rooms were in use. From here the main staircase continued up to the second floor, where were situated certain bedrooms, one of which I occupied, while on the other side of the first-floor landing some half-dozen steps led to another suite of rooms, where, at the time I am speaking of, Arthur Inglis, the artist, had his bedroom and studio. Thus the landing outside my bedroom, at the top of the house, commanded both the landing of the first floor, and also the steps that led to Inglis' rooms. Jim Stanley and his wife, finally (whose guest I was), occupied rooms in another wing of the house, where also were the servants' quarters.

I arrived just in time for lunch on a brilliant noon of mid-May. The garden was shouting with color and fragrance, and not less delightful, after my broiling walk up from the *marina*, should have been the coming from the reverberating heat and blaze of the day into the marble coolness of the villa. Only (the reader has my bare word for this, and nothing more), the moment I set foot in the house I felt that something was wrong. This feeling, I may say, was quite vague, though very strong, and I remember that when I saw letters waiting for me on the table in the hall I felt certain that the explanation was here: I was convinced that there was bad news of some sort for me. Yet when I opened them I found no such explanation of my premonition: my correspondents all reeked of prosperity. Yet this clear miscarriage of a presentiment did not dissipate my uneasiness. In that cool fragrant house there was something wrong.

I am at pains to mention this because it may explain why it was that, though I am as a rule so excellent a sleeper that the extinction of a light on getting into bed is apparently contemporaneous with being called on the following morning, I slept very badly on my first night in the Villa

Casana. It may also explain the fact that when I did sleep (if it was indeed in sleep that I saw what I thought I saw) I dreamed in a very vivid and original manner, original, that is to say, in the sense that something which, as far as I knew, had never previously entered into my consciousness, usurped it then. But since, in addition to this evil premonition, certain words and events occurring during the rest of the day, might have suggested something of what I thought happened that night, it will be well to relate them.

After lunch, then, I went round the house with Mrs. Stanley, and during our tour she referred, it is true, to the unoccupied bedroom on the first floor, which opened out of the room where we had lunched.

"We left that unoccupied," she said, "because Jim and I have a charming bedroom and dressing room, as you saw, in the wing, and if we used it ourselves we should have to turn the dining room into a dressing room and have our meals downstairs. As it is, however, we have our little flat there, Arthur Inglis has his little flat in the other passage; and I remembered (aren't I extraordinary?) that you once said that the higher up you were in a house the better you were pleased. So I put you at the top of the house, instead of giving you that room."

It is true that a doubt, vague as my uneasy premonition, crossed my mind at this. I did not see why Mrs. Stanley should have explained all this, if there had not been more to explain. I allow, therefore, that the thought that there was something to explain about the unoccupied bedroom was momentarily present to my mind.

The second thing that may have borne on my dream was this.

At dinner the conversation turned for a moment on ghosts. Inglis, with the certainty of conviction, expressed his belief that anybody who could possibly believe in the existence of supernatural phenomena was unworthy of the name of a fool. The subject instantly dropped. As far as I can recollect, nothing else occurred or was said that could bear on what follows.

We all went to bed rather early, and personally I yawned my way upstairs, feeling hideously sleepy. My room was rather hot, and I threw all the windows wide, and from without poured in the white light of the moon, and the love song of many nightingales. I undressed quickly, and got into bed, but though I had felt so sleepy before, I now felt extremely wide-awake. But I was quite content to be awake: I did not toss or turn, I felt perfectly happy listening to the song and seeing the light. Then, it is possible, I may have gone to sleep, and what follows may have been a dream. I thought anyhow that after a time the nightingales ceased singing and the moon sank. I thought also that if, for some unexplained reason, I was going to lie awake all night, I might as well read, and I remembered that I had left a book in which I was interested in the dining room on the first floor. So I got out of bed, lit a candle, and went downstairs. I entered the room, saw on a side table the book I had come to look for, and then, simultaneously, saw that the door into the unoccupied bedroom was open. A curious gray light not of dawn nor of moonshine, came out of it, and I looked in. The bed stood just opposite the door, a big four-poster, hung with tapestry at the head. Then I saw that the grayish light of the bedroom came from the bed, or rather from what was on the bed. For it was covered with great caterpillars, a foot or more in length, which crawled over it. They were faintly luminous, and it was the light from them that showed me the room. Instead of the sucker-feet of ordinary caterpillars they had rows of pincers like crabs, and they moved by grasping what they lay on with their pincers, and then sliding their bodies forward. In color these dreadful insects were yellowish gray, and they were covered with irregular lumps and swellings. There must have been hundreds of them, for they formed a sort of writhing, crawling pyramid on the bed. Occasionally one fell off onto the floor, with a soft fleshy thud, and though the floor was of hard concrete, it yielded to the pincer-feet as if it had been putty, and crawling back, the caterpillar would mount on to the bed again, to rejoin its fearful companions. They appeared to have no faces, so to speak, but at one end of them there was a mouth that opened sideways in respiration.

Then, as I looked, it seemed to me as if they all suddenly became conscious of my presence. All the mouths at any rate were turned in my direction, and the next moment they began dropping off the bed with those soft fleshy thuds onto the floor, and wriggling towards me. For one second the paralysis of nightmare was on me, but the next I was running upstairs again to my room, and I remember feeling the cold of the marble steps on my bare feet. I rushed into my bedroom, and slammed the door behind me, and then—I was certainly wide-awake now—I found myself standing by my bed with the sweat of terror pouring from me. The noise of the banged door still rang in my ears. But, as would have been more usual, if this had been mere nightmare, the terror that had been mine when I saw those foul beasts crawling about the bed or dropping softly onto the floor did not cease then. Awake now, if dreaming before, I did not at all recover from the horror of dream: it did not seem to me that I had dreamed. And until dawn, I sat or stood, not daring to lie down, thinking that every rustle or movement that I heard was the approach of the caterpillars. To them and the claws that bit into the cement, the wood of the door was child's play: steel would not keep them out.

But with the sweet and noble return of day the horror vanished: the whisper of wind became benignant again: the nameless fear, whatever it was, was smoothed out and terrified me no longer. Dawn broke, hueless at first; then it grew dove-colored, then the flaming pageant of light spread over the sky.

The admirable rule of the house was that everybody had breakfast where and when he pleased, and in consequence it was not till lunch-time that I met any of the other members of our party, since I had breakfast on my balcony, and wrote letters and other things till lunch. In fact, I got down to that meal rather late, after the other three had begun. Between my knife and fork there was a small pillbox of cardboard, and as I sat down Inglis spoke.

"Do look at that," he said, "since you are interested in natural history. I found it crawling on my counterpane last night, and I don't know what it is."

I think that before I opened the pillbox I expected something of the sort which I found in it. Inside it, anyhow, was a small caterpillar, grayish-yellow in color, with curious bumps and excrescences on its rings. It was extremely active, and hurried round the box, this way and that. Its feet were unlike the feet of any caterpillar I ever saw: they were like the pincers of a crab. I looked, and shut the lid down again.

"No, I don't know it," I said, "but it looks rather unwholesome. What are you going to do with it?"

"Oh, I shall keep it," said Inglis. "It has begun to spin: I want to see what sort of a moth it turns into."

I opened the box again, and saw that these hurrying movements were indeed the beginning of the spinning of the web of its cocoon. Then Inglis spoke again.

"It has got funny feet, too," he said. "They are like crabs' pincers. What's the Latin for crab? Oh, yes, Cancer. So in case it is unique, let's christen it: 'Cancer Inglisensis.'"

Then something happened in my brain, some momentary piecing together of all that I had seen or dreamed. Something in his words seemed to me to throw light on it all, and my own intense horror at the experience of the night before linked itself onto what he had just said. In effect, I took the box and threw it, caterpillar and all, out of the window. There was a gravel path just outside, and beyond it a fountain playing into a basin. The box fell onto the middle of this.

Inglis laughed.

"So the students of the occult don't like solid facts," he said. "My poor caterpillar!"

The talk went off again at once on to other subjects, and I have only given in detail, as they happened, these trivialities in order to be sure myself that I have recorded everything that could have borne on occult subjects or on the subject of caterpillars. But at the moment when I threw the pillbox into the fountain, I lost my head: my only excuse is that, as is probably plain, the tenant of it was, in miniature, exactly what I had seen crowded onto the bed in the unoccupied room. And though this translation of those phantoms into flesh and blood—or whatever it is that caterpillars are made of—ought perhaps to have relieved the horror of the night, as a matter of fact it did nothing of the kind. It only made the crawling pyramid that covered the bed in the unoccupied room more hideously real.

After lunch we spent a lazy hour or two strolling about the garden or sitting in the *loggia*, and it must have been about four o'clock when Stanley and I started off to bathe, down that path that led by the fountain into which I had thrown the pillbox. The water was shallow and clear, and at the bottom of it I saw its white remains. The soaking had disintegrated the cardboard, and it had become no more than a few strips and shreds of sodden paper. The center of the fountain was a marble Italian Cupid which squirted the water out of a wineskin held under its arm. And crawling up its leg was the caterpillar. Strange and scarcely credible as it seemed, it must have survived the falling-to-bits of its prison, and made its way to shore, and there it was, out of arm's reach, weaving and waving this way and that as it evolved its cocoon.

Then, as I looked at it, it seemed to me again that, like the caterpillars I had seen last night, it saw me, and breaking out of the threads that surrounded it, it crawled down the marble leg of the Cupid and began swimming like a snake across the water of the fountain towards me. It came with extraordinary speed (the fact of a caterpillar being able to swim was new to me), and in another moment was crawling up the marble lip of the basin. Just then Inglis joined us.

"Why, if it isn't old 'Cancer Inglisensis' again," he said, catching sight of the beast. "What a tearing hurry it is in."

We were standing side by side on the path, and when the caterpillar had advanced to within about a yard of us, it stopped, and began waving again, as if in doubt as to the direction in which it should go. Then it appeared to make up its mind, and crawled onto Inglis' shoe.

"It likes me best," he said, "but I don't really know that I like it. And as it won't drown I think perhaps—"

He shook it off his shoe onto the gravel path and trod on it.

All the afternoon the air got heavier and heavier with the sirocco that was without doubt coming up from the south, and that night again I went up to bed feeling very sleepy, but below my drowsiness, so to speak, there was the consciousness, stronger than before, that there was something wrong in the house, that something dangerous was close at hand. But I fell asleep at once, and—how long after I do not know—either woke or dreamed I awoke, feeling that I must get up at once, *or I should be too late.* Then (dreaming or awake) I lay and fought this fear, telling myself that I was but the prey of my own nerves disordered by sirocco or what not, and at the same time quite clearly knowing in another part of my mind, so to speak, that every moment's delay added to the danger. At last this second feeling became irresistible, and I put on coat and trousers and went out of my room onto the landing. And then I saw that I had already delayed too long, and that I was now too late.

The whole of the landing of the first floor below was invisible under the swarm of caterpillars that crawled there. The folding doors into the sitting room from which opened the bedroom where I had seen them last night, were shut, but they were squeezing through the cracks of it, and dropping one by one through the keyhole, elongating themselves into mere string as they passed, and growing fat and lumpy again on emerging. Some, as if exploring, were nosing about the steps into the passage at the end of which were Inglis' rooms, others were crawling on the lowest steps of the staircase that led up to where I stood. The landing, however, was completely covered with them: I was cut off. And of the frozen horror that seized me when I saw that, I can give no idea in words.

Then at last a general movement began to take place, and they grew thicker on the steps that led to Inglis' room. Gradually, like some hideous tide of flesh, they advanced along the passage, and I saw the foremost, visible by the pale gray luminousness that came from them, reach his door. Again and again I tried to shout and warn him, in terror all the time that they should turn at the sound of my voice and mount my stair instead, but for all my efforts I felt that no sound came from my throat. They crawled along the hinge-crack of his door, passing through as they had done before, and still I stood there making impotent efforts to shout to him, to bid him escape while there was time.

At last the passage was completely empty: they had all gone, and at that moment I was conscious for the first time of the cold of the marble landing on which I stood barefooted. The dawn was just beginning to break in the eastern sky.

Six months later I met Mrs. Stanley in a country house in England. We talked on many subjects, and at last she said:

"I don't think I have seen you since I got that dreadful news about Arthur Inglis a month ago."

"I haven't heard," said I.

"No? He has got cancer. They don't even advise an operation, for there is no hope of a cure; he is riddled with it, the doctors say."

Now during all these six months I do not think a day had passed on which I had not had in my mind the dreams (or whatever you like to call them) which I had seen in the Villa Casana.

"It is awful, is it not?" she continued, "and I feel, I can't help feeling, that he may have—"

"Caught it at the villa?" I asked.

She looked at me in blank surprise.

"Why did you say that?" she asked. "How did you know?"

Then she told me. In the unoccupied bedroom a year before there had been a fatal case of cancer. She had, of course, taken the best advice and had been told that the utmost dictates of prudence would be obeyed as long as she did not put anybody to sleep in the room, which had also been thoroughly disinfected and newly whitewashed and painted. But—

Bram Stoker

The Squaw

Nuremberg at the time was not so much exploited as it has been since then. Irving had not been playing *Faust,* and the very name of the old town was hardly known to the great bulk of the traveling public. My wife and I being in the second week of our honeymoon, naturally wanted someone else to join our party, so that when the cheery stranger, Elias P. Hutcheson, hailing from Isthmain City, Bleeding Gulch, Maple Tree County, Neb., turned up at the station at Frankfurt, and casually remarked that he was going on to see the most all-fired old Methuselah of a town in Europe, and that he guessed that so much traveling alone was enough to send an intelligent, active citizen into the melancholy ward of a daft house, we took the pretty broad hint and suggested that we should join forces. We found, on comparing notes afterwards, that we had each intended to speak with some diffidence or hesitation so as not to appear too eager, such not being a good compliment to the success of our married life; but the effect was entirely marred by our both beginning to speak at the same instant—stopping simultaneously and then going on together again. Anyhow, no matter how, it was done; and Elias P. Hutcheson became one of our party. Straightaway Amelia and I found the pleasant benefit; instead of quarreling, as we had been doing, we found that the restraining influence of a third party was such that we now took every opportunity of spooning in odd corners. Amelia declares that ever since she has, as the result of that experience, advised all her friends to take a friend on the honeymoon. Well, we "did" Nuremberg together, and much enjoyed the racy remarks of our transatlantic friend, who, from his quaint speech and his wonderful stock of adventures, might have stepped out of a novel. We kept for the last object of interest in the city to be visited the Burg, and on the day appointed for the visit strolled round the outer wall of the city by the eastern side.

The Burg is seated on a rock dominating the town, and an immensely deep fosse guards it on the northern side. Nuremberg has been happy in that it was never sacked; had it been it would certainly not be so spick-and-span perfect as it is at present. The ditch has not been used for centuries, and now its base is spread with tea gardens and orchards, of which some of the trees are of quite respectable growth. As we wandered round the wall, dawdling in the hot July sunshine, we often paused to admire the views spread before us, and in especial the great plain covered with towns and villages and bounded with a blue line of hills, like a landscape of Claude Lorraine. From this we always turned with new delight to the city itself, with its myriad of quaint old gables and acre-wide red roofs dotted with dormer windows, tier upon tier. A little to our right rose the towers of the Burg, and nearer still, standing grim, the Torture Tower, which was, and is, perhaps, the most interesting place in the city. For centuries the tradition of the Iron Virgin of Nuremberg has been handed down as an instance of the horrors of cruelty of which man is capable; we had long looked forward to seeing it; and here at last was its home.

In one of our pauses we leaned over the wall of the moat and looked down. The garden seemed quite fifty or sixty feet below us, and the sun pouring into it with an intense, moveless heat like that of an oven. Beyond rose the gray, grim wall seemingly of endless height, and losing itself right and left in the angles of bastion and counterscarp. Trees and bushes crowned the wall, and above again towered the lofty houses on whose massive beauty Time has only set the hand of approval. The sun was hot and we were lazy; time was our own, and we lingered, leaning on the wall. Just below us was a pretty sight—a great black cat lying stretched in the sun, whilst round her gamboled prettily a tiny black kitten. The mother would wave her tail for the kitten to play with, or would raise her feet and push away the little one as an encouragement to further play. They were just at the foot of the wall, and Elias P. Hutcheson, in order to help the play, stooped and took from the walk a moderate-sized pebble.

"See!" he said, "I will drop it near the kitten, and they will both wonder where it came from."

"Oh, be careful," said my wife; "you might hit the dear little thing!"

"Not me, ma'am," said Elias P. "Why, I'm as tender as a Maine cherry tree. Lord, bless ye, I wouldn't hurt the poor pooty little critter more'n I'd scalp a baby. An' you may bet your variegated socks on that! See, I'll drop it fur away on the outside so's not to go near her!" Thus saying, he leaned over and held his arm out at full length and dropped the stone. It may be that there is some attractive force which draws lesser matters to greater; or more probably that the wall was not plumb but sloped to its base—we not noticing the inclination from above; but the stone fell with a sickening thud that came up to us through the hot air, right on the kitten's head, and shattered out its little brains then and there. The black cat cast a swift upward glance, and we saw her eyes like green fire fixed an instant on Elias P. Hutcheson; and then her attention was given to the kitten, which lay still with just a quiver of her tiny limbs, whilst a thin red stream trickled from a gaping wound. With a muffled cry, such as a human being might give, she bent over the kitten, licking its wound and moaning. Suddenly she seemed to realize that it was dead, and again threw her eyes up at us. I shall never forget the sight, for she looked the perfect incarnation of hate. Her green eyes blazed with lurid fire, and the white, sharp teeth seemed to almost shine through the blood which dabbled her mouth and whiskers. She gnashed her teeth, and her claws stood out stark and at full length on every paw. Then she made a wild rush up the wall as if to reach us, but when the momentum ended fell back, and further added to her horrible appearance for she fell on the kitten, and rose with her back fur smeared with its brains and blood. Amelia turned quite faint, and I had to lift her back from the wall. There was a seat close by in shade of a spreading plane tree, and here I placed her whilst she composed herself. Then I went back to Hutcheson, who stood without moving, looking down on the angry cat below.

As I joined him, he said:

"Well, I guess that air the savagest beast I ever see—'cept once when an Apache squaw had an edge on a half-breed what they nicknamed 'Splinters' 'cos of the way he fixed up her papoose which he stole on a raid just to show that he appreciated the way they had given his mother the fire torture. She got that kinder look so set on her face that it just seemed to grow there. She followed Splinters more'n three years till at last the braves got him and handed him over to her. They did say that no man, white or Injun, had ever been so long a-dying under the tortures of the Apaches. The only time I ever see her smile was when I wiped her out. I kem on the camp just in time to see Splinters pass in his checks, and he wasn't sorry to go either. He was a hard citizen, and though I never could shake with him after that papoose business—for it was bitter bad, and he should have been a white man, for he looked like one—I see he had got paid out in full. Durn me, but I took a piece of his hide from one of his skinnin posts an' had it made into a pocketbook. It's here now!" and he slapped the breast pocket of his coat.

Whilst he was speaking the cat was continuing her frantic efforts to get up the wall. She would take a run back and then charge up, sometimes reaching an incredible height. She did not seem to mind the heavy fall which she got each time but started with renewed vigor; and at every tumble her appearance became more horrible. Hutcheson was a kind-hearted man—my wife and I had both noticed little acts of kindness to animals as well as to persons—and he seemed concerned at the state of fury to which the cat had wrought herself.

"Well now!" he said. "I do declare that the poor critter seems quite desperate. There, there, poor thing, it was all an accident—though that won't bring back your little one to you. Say! I wouldn't have had such a thing happen for a thousand! Just shows what a clumsy fool of a man can do when he tries to play! Seems I'm too darned slipper-handed to even play with a cat. Say, Colonel!"—it was a pleasant way he had to bestow titles freely—"I hope your wife don't hold no grudge against me on account of this unpleasantness? Why, I wouldn't have had it occur on no account."

He came over to Amelia and apologized profusely, and she with her usual kindness of heart hastened to assure him that she quite understood that it was an accident. Then we all went again to the wall and looked over.

The cat, missing Hutcheson's face, had drawn back across the moat, and was sitting on her haunches as though ready to spring. Indeed, the very instant she saw him she did spring, and with a blind unreasoning fury, which would have been grotesque, only that it was so frightfully real. She did not try to run up the wall, but simply launched herself at him as though hate and fury could lend her wings to pass straight through the great distance between them. Amelia, womanlike, got quite concerned, and said to Elias P. in a warning voice:

"Oh, you must be very careful. That animal would try to kill you if she were here; her eyes look like positive murder."

He laughed out jovially. "Excuse me, ma'am," he said, "but I can't help laughin'. Fancy a man that has fought grizzlies an' Injuns bein' careful of bein' murdered by a cat!"

When the cat heard him laugh, her whole demeanor seemed to change. She no longer tried to jump or run up the wall, but went quietly over, and sitting again beside the dead kitten began to lick and fondle it as though it were alive.

"See," said I, "the effect of a really strong man. Even that animal in the midst of her fury recognizes the voice of a master, and bows to him!"

"Like a squaw!" was the only comment of Elias P. Hutcheson, as we moved on our way round the city fosse. Every now and then we looked over the wall and each time saw the cat following us. At first she had kept going back to the dead kitten, and then as the distance grew greater took it in her mouth and so followed. After a while, however, she abandoned this, for we saw her following all alone; she had evidently hidden the body somewhere. Amelia's alarm grew at the cat's persistence, and more than once she repeated her warning; but the American always laughed with amusement, till finally, seeing that she was beginning to be worried, he said:

"I say, ma'am, you needn't be skeered over that cat. I go heeled, I do!" Here he slapped his pistol pocket at the back of his lumbar region. "Why, sooner'n have you worried, I'll shoot the critter, right here, an' risk the police interferin' with a citizen of the United States for carryin' arms contrairy to reg'lations!" As he spoke he looked over the wall, but the cat, on seeing him, retreated, with a growl, into a bed of tall flowers, and was hidden. He went on: "Blest if that ar critter ain't got more sense of what's good for her than most Christians. I guess we've seen the last of her! You bet, she'll go back now to that busted kitten and have a private funeral of it, all to herself!"

Amelia did not like to say more, lest he might, in mistaken kindness to her, fulfill his threat of shooting the cat: and so we went on and crossed the little wooden bridge leading to the gateway whence ran the steep paved roadway between the

Burg and the pentagonal Torture Tower. As we crossed the bridge we saw the cat again down below us. When she saw us her fury seemed to return, and she made frantic efforts to get up the steep wall. Hutcheson laughed as he looked down at her, and said:

"Good-bye, old girl. Sorry I injured your feelin's, but you'll get over it in time! So long!" And then we passed through the long, dim archway and came to the gate of the Burg.

When we came out again after our survey of this most beautiful old place which not even the well-intended efforts of the Gothic restorers of forty years ago have been able to spoil—though their restoration was then glaring white—we seemed to have quite forgotten the unpleasant episode of the morning. The old lime tree with its great trunk gnarled with the passing of nearly nine centuries, the deep well cut through the heart of the rock by those captives of old, and the lovely view from the city wall whence we heard, spread over almost a full quarter of an hour, the multitudinous chimes of the city, had all helped to wipe out from our minds the incident of the slain kitten.

We were the only visitors who had entered the Torture Tower that morning—so at least said the old custodian—and as we had the place all to ourselves were able to make a minute and more satisfactory survey than would have otherwise been possible. The custodian, looking to us as the sole source of his gains for the day, was willing to meet our wishes in any way. The Torture Tower is truly a grim place, even now when many thousands of visitors have sent a stream of life, and the joy that follows life, into the place; but at the time I mention, it wore its grimmest and most gruesome aspect. The dust of ages seemed to have settled on it, and the darkness and the horror of its memories seem to have become sentient in a way that would have satisfied the Pantheistic souls of Philo or Spinoza. The lower chamber where we entered was seemingly, in its normal state, filled with incarnate darkness; even the hot sunlight streaming in through the door seemed to be lost in the vast thickness of the walls, and only showed the masonry rough as when the builder's scaffolding had come down, but coated with dust and marked here and there with patches of dark stain which, if walls could speak, could have given their own dread memories of fear and pain. We were glad to pass up the dusty wooden staircase, the custodian leaving the outer door open to light us somewhat on our way; for to our eyes the one long-wick'd, evil-smelling candle stuck in a sconce on the wall gave an inadequate light. When we came up through the open trap in the corner of the chamber overhead, Amelia held on to me so tightly that I could actually feel her heart beat. I must say for my own part that I was not surprised at her fear, for this room was even more gruesome than that below. Here there was certainly more light, but only just sufficient to realize the horrible surroundings of the place. The builders of the tower had evidently intended that only they who should gain the top should have any of the joys of light and propsect. There, as we had noticed from below, were ranges of windows, albeit of medieval smallness, but elsewhere in the tower were only a very few narrow slits such as were habitual in places of medieval defense. A few of these only lit the chamber, and these so high up in the wall that from no part could the sky be seen through the thickness of the walls. In racks, and leaning in disorder against the walls, were a number of headsmen's swords, great double-handed weapons with broad blade and keen edge. Hard by were several blocks whereon the necks of the victims had lain, with here and there deep notches where the steel had bitten through the guard of flesh and shored into the wood. Round the chamber, placed in all sorts of irregular ways, were many implements of torture which made one's heart ache to see—chairs full of spikes which gave instant and excruciating pain; chairs and couches with dull knobs whose torture was seemingly less, but which, though slower, were equally efficacious; racks, belts, boots, gloves, collars, all made for compressing at will; steel baskets in which the head could be slowly crushed into a pulp if necessary; watchmen's hooks with long handle and knife that cut at resistance—this a specialty of the old Nuremberg police system; and many, many other devices for man's injury to man. Amelia grew quite pale with the horror of the things, but fortunately did not faint, for being a little overcome she sat down on a torture chair, but jumped up again with a shriek, all tendency to faint gone. We both pretended that it was the injury done to her dress by the dust of the chair, and the rusty spikes which had upset her, and Mr. Hutcheson acquiesced in accepting the explanation with a kind-hearted laugh.

But the central object in the whole of this chamber of horrors was the engine known as the Iron Virgin, which stood near the center of the room. It was a rudely-shaped figure of a woman, something of the bell order, or, to make a closer comparison, of the figure of Mrs. Noah in the children's Ark, but without that slimness of waist and perfect *rondeur* of hip which marks the aesthetic type of the Noah family. One would hardly have recognized it as intended for a human figure at all had not the founder shaped on the forehead a rude semblance of a woman's face. This machine was coated with rust without, and covered with dust; a rope was fastened to a ring in the front of the figure, about where the waist should have been, and was drawn through a pulley, fastened on the wooden pillar which sustained the flooring above. The custodian pulling this rope showed that a section of the front was hinged like a door at one side; we then saw that the engine was of considerable thickness, leaving just room enough inside for a man to be placed. The door was of equal thickness and of great weight, for it took the custodian all his strength, aided though he was by the contrivance of the pulley, to open it. This weight was partly due to the fact that the door was of manifest purpose hung so as to throw its weight downwards, so that it might shut of its own accord when the strain was released. The inside was honeycombed with rust—nay more, the rust alone that comes through time would hardly have eaten so deep into the iron walls; the rust of the cruel stains was deep indeed! It was only, however, when we came to look at the inside of the door that the diabolical intention was manifest to the full. Here were several long spikes, square and massive, broad at the base and sharp at the point, placed in such a position that when the door should close the upper ones would pierce the eyes of the victim, and the lower ones his heart and vitals. The sight was too much for poor Amelia, and this time she fainted dead off, and I had to carry her down the stairs, and place her on a bench outside till she recovered. That she felt it to the quick was afterwards shown by the fact that my eldest son bears to this day a rude birthmark on his breast, which has, by family consent, been accepted as representing the Nuremberg Virgin.

When we got back to the chamber we found Hutcheson still opposite the Iron Virgin; he had been evidently philosophizing, and now gave us the benefit of his thought in the shape of a sort of exordium.

"Well, I guess I've been learnin' somethin' here while madam has been gettin' over her faint. 'Pears to me that we're a long way behind the times on our side of the big drink. We uster think out on the plains that the Injun could give us points in tryin' to make a man uncomfortable; but I guess your old medieval law-and-order party could raise him every time. Splinters was pretty good in his bluff on the squaw, but this here young miss held a straight flush all high on him. The points of them spikes air sharp enough still, though even the edges air eaten out by what uster be on them. It'd be a good thing for our

Indian section to get some specimens of this here play toy to send round to the reservations jest to knock the stuffin' out of the bucks, and the squaws too, by showing them as how old civilization lays over them at their best. Guess but I'll get in that box a minute jest to see how it feels!"

"Oh no! no!" said Amelia. "It is too terrible!"

"Guess, ma'am, nothin's too terrible to the explorin' mind. I've been in some queer places in my time. Spent a night inside a dead horse while a prairie fire swept over me in Montana Territory—an' another time slept inside a dead buffalo when the Comanches was on the warpath an' I didn't keer to leave my kyard on them. I've been two days in a caved-in tunnel in the Billy Broncho gold mine in New Mexico, an' was one of the four shut up for three parts of a day in the caisson what slid over on her side when we was settin' the foundations of the Buffalo Bridge. I've not funked an odd experience yet, an' I don't propose to begin now!"

We saw that he was set on the experiment, so I said: "Well, hurry up, old man, and get through it quick?"

"All right, General," said he, "but I calculate we ain't quite ready yet. The gentlemen, my predecessors, what stood in that thar canister, didn't volunteer for the office—not much! And I guess there was some ornamental tyin' up before the big stroke was made. I want to go into this thing fair and square, so I must get fixed up proper first. I dare say this old galoot can rise some string and tie me up accordin' to sample?"

This was said interrogatively to the old custodian, but the latter, who understood the drift of his speech, though perhaps not appreciating to the full the niceties of dialect and imagery, shook his head. His protest was, however, only formal and made to be overcome. The American thrust a gold piece into his hand, saying, "Take it, pard! It's your pot; and don't be skeer'd. This ain't no necktie party that you're asked to assist in!" He produced some thin frayed rope and proceeded to bind our companion, with sufficient strictness for the purpose. When the upper part of his body was bound, Hutcheson said:

"Hold on a moment, Judge. Guess I'm too heavy for you to tote into the canister. You just let me walk in, and then you can wash up regardin' my legs!"

Whilst speaking he had backed himself into the opening which was just enough to hold him. It was a close fit and no mistake. Amelia looked on with fear in her eyes, but she evidently did not like to say anything. Then the custodian completed his task by tying the American's feet together so that he was now absolutely helpless and fixed in his voluntary prison. He seemed to really enjoy it, and the incipient smile which was habitual to his face blossomed into actuality as he said:

"Guess this here Eve was made out of the rib of a dwarf! There ain't much room for a full-grown citizen of the United States to hustle. We uster make our coffins more roomier in Idaho territory. Now, Judge, you just begin to let this door down, slow, on to me. I want to feel the same pleasure as the other jays had when those spikes began to move towards their eyes!''

"Oh no! no! no!'' broke Amelia hysterically. "It is too terrible! I can't bear to see it!—I cant! I can't''

But the American was obdurate. "Say, Colonel,'' said he, "Why not take Madame for a little promenade? I wouldn't hurt her feelin's for the world; but now that I am here, havin' kem eight thousand miles, wouldn't it be too hard to give up the very experience I've been pinin' an' pantin' fur? A man can't get to feel like canned goods every time! Me and the Judge here'll fix up this thing in no time, an' then you'll come back, an' we'll all laugh together!''

Once more the resolution that is born of curiosity triumphed, and Amelia stayed holding tight to my arm and shivering whilst the custodian began to slacken slowly inch by inch the rope that held back the iron door. Hutcheson's face was positively radiant as his eyes followed the first movement of the spikes.

"Well!'' he said, "I guess I've not had enjoyment like this since I left New York. Bar a scrap with a French sailor at Wapping—an' that warn't much of a picnic neither—I've not had a show fur real pleasure in this dod-rotted Continent, where there ain't no bars nor no Injuns, an' where nary a man goes heeled. Slow there, Judge! Don't you rush this business! I want a show for my money this game—I do!''

The custodian must have had in him some of the blood of his predecessors in that ghastly tower, for he worked the engine with a deliberate and excruciating slowness which after five minutes, in which the outer edge of the door had not moved half as many inches, began to overcome Amelia. I saw her lips whiten, and I felt her hold upon my arm relax. I looked around an instant for a place whereon to lay her, and when I looked at her again found that her eye had become fixed on the side of the Virgin. Following its direction I saw the black cat crouching out of sight. Her green eyes shone like danger lamps in the gloom of the place, and their color was heightened by the blood which still smeared her coat and reddened her mouth. I cried out:

"The cat! Look out for the cat!" For even then she sprang out before the engine. At this moment she looked like a triumphant demon. Her eyes blazed with ferocity, her hair bristled out till she seemed twice her normal size, and her tail lashed about as does a tiger's when the quarry is before it. Elias P. Hutcheson when he saw her was amused, and his eyes positively sparkled with fun as he said:

"Darned if the squaw hain't got on all her war paint! Jest give her a shove off if she comes any of her tricks on me, for I'm so fixed everlastingly by the boss, that durn my skin if I can keep my eyes from her if she wants them! Easy there, Judge! Don't you slack that ar rope or I'm euchered!"

At this moment Amelia completed her faint, and I had to clutch hold of her round the waist or she would have fallen to the floor. Whilst attending to her I saw the black cat crouching for a spring, and jumped up to turn the creature out.

But at that instant, with a sort of hellish scream, she hurled herself, not as we expected at Hutcheson, but straight at the face of the custodian. Her claws seemed to be tearing wildly as one sees in the Chinese drawings of the dragon rampant, and as I looked I saw one of them light on the poor man's eye, and actually tear through it and down his cheek, leaving a wide band of red where the blood seemed to spurt from every vein.

With a yell of sheer terror which came quicker than even his sense of pain, the man leaped back, dropping as he did so the rope which held back the iron door. I jumped for it but was too late, for the cord ran like lightning through the pulley-block, and the heavy mass fell forward from its own weight.

As the door closed I caught a glimpse of our poor companion's face. He seemed frozen with terror. His eyes stared with a horrible anguish as if dazed, and no sound came from his lips.

And when the spikes did their work. Happily the end was quick, for when I wrenched open the door they had pierced so deep that they had locked in the bones of the skull through which they had crushed and actually tore him—it—out of his iron prison till, bound as he was, he fell at full length with a sickly thud upon the floor, the face turning upwards as he fell.

I rushed to my wife, lifted her up and carried her out, for I feared for her very reason if she should wake from her faint to such a scene. I laid her on the bench outside and ran back.

Leaning against the wooden column was the custodian moaning in pain whilst he held his reddening handkerchief to his eyes. And sitting on the head of the poor American was the cat, purring loudly as she licked the blood which trickled through the gashed sockets of his eyes.

I think no one will call me cruel because I seized one of the old executioner's swords and shore her in two as she sat.

Guy de Maupassant

The Hand

They made a circle around Judge Bermutier, who was giving his opinion of the mysterious affair that had happened at Saint-Cloud. For a month Paris had doted on this inexplicable crime. No one could understand it at all.

M. Bermutier, standing with his back to the chimney, talked about it, discussed the divers opinions but came to no conclusions.

Many women had risen and come nearer, remaining standing, with eyes fixed upon the shaven mouth of the magistrate whence issued these grave words. They shivered and vibrated, crisp through their curious fear, through that eager, insatiable need of terror which haunts their soul, torturing them like a hunger.

One of them, paler than the others, after a silence, said:

"It is frightful. It touches the supernatural. We shall never know anything about it."

The magistrate turned toward her, saying:

"Yes, madame, it is probable that we never shall know anything about it. As for the word 'supernatural,' when you come to use that, it has no place here. We are in the presence of a crime skillfully conceived, very skillfully executed and so well enveloped in mystery that we cannot separate the impenetrable circumstances which surround it. But once in my life I had to follow an affair which seemed truly to be mixed up with something very unusual. However, it was necessary to give it up, as there was no means of explaining it."

Many of the ladies called out at the same time, so quickly that their voices sounded as one:

"Oh, tell us about it."

M. Bermutier smiled gravely, as judges should, and replied:

"You must not suppose, for an instant, that I, at least, believed there was anything superhuman in the adventure. I believe only in normal causes. And if in place of using the word 'supernatural' to express what we cannot comprehend we should simply use the word 'inexplicable,' it would be much better. In any case, the surrounding circumstances in the affair I am going to relate to you, as well as the preparatory circumstances, have affected me much. Here are the facts:

"I was then judge of instruction at Ajaccio, a little white town lying on the border of an admirable gulf that was surrounded on all sides by high mountains.

"What I particularly had to look after there were the affairs of vendetta. Some of them were superb, as dramatic as possible, ferocious and heroic. We find there the most beautiful subjects of vengeance that one could dream of, hatred a century old, appeased for a moment but never extinguished, abominable plots, assassinations becoming massacres and almost glorious battles. For two years I heard of nothing but the price of blood, of the terribly prejudiced Corsican who is bound to avenge all injury upon the person of him who is the cause of it or upon his nearest descendants. I saw old men and infants, cousins, with their throats cut, and my head was full of these stories.

"One day we learned that an Englishman had rented for some years a little villa at the end of the gulf. He had brought with him a French domestic, picked up at Marseilles on the way.

"Soon everybody was occupied with this singular person who lived alone in his house, only going out to hunt and fish. He spoke to no one, never came to the town and every morning practiced shooting with a pistol and a rifle for an hour or two.

"Some legends about him were abroad. They pretended that he was a high personage fled from his own country for political reasons; then they affirmed that he was concealing himself after having committed a frightful crime. They even cited some of the particularly horrible details.

"In my capacity of judge I wished to get some information about this man. But it was impossible to learn anything. He called himself Sir John Rowell.

"I contented myself with watching him closely, although in reality there seemed nothing to suspect regarding him.

"Nevertheless, as rumors on his account continued, grew and became general, I resolved to try and see this stranger myself and for this purpose began to hunt regularly in the neighborhood of his property.

"I waited long for an occasion. It finally came in the form of a partridge which I shot and killed before the very nose of the Englishman. My dog brought it to me, but, immediately taking it, I went and begged Sir John Rowell to accept the dead bird, excusing myself for intrusion.

"He was a tall man with red hair and red beard, very large, a sort of placid, polite Hercules. He had none of the so-called British haughtiness and heartily thanked me for the delicacy in French, with a beyond-the-Channel accent. At the end of a month we had chatted together five or six times.

"Finally one evening, as I was passing by his door, I perceived him astride a chair in the garden, smoking his pipe. I saluted him and he asked me in to have a glass of beer. It was not necessary for him to repeat before I accepted.

"He received me with the fastidious courtesy of the English, spoke in praise of France and of Corsica and declared that he loved that country and that shore.

"Then with great precaution in the form of a lively interest, I put some questions to him about his life and his projects. He responded without embarrassment, told me that he had traveled much, in Africa, in the Indies, and in America. He added, laughing:

"'I have had many adventures, oh yes!'

"I began to talk about hunting, and he gave me many curious details of hunting the hippopotamus, the tiger, the elephant, and even of hunting the gorilla.

"I said: 'All these animals are very formidable.'

"He laughed. 'Oh no! The worst animal is man.' Then he began to laugh with the hearty laugh of a big, contented Englishman. He continued:

"'I have often hunted man also.'

"He spoke of weapons and asked me to go into his house to see his guns of various makes and kinds.

"His drawing room was hung in black, in black silk embroidered in gold. There were great yellow flowers running over the somber stuff, shining like fire.

"'It is Japanese cloth,' he said.

"But in the middle of a large panel a strange thing attracted my eye. Upon a square of red velvet a black object was attached. I approached and found it was a hand, the hand of a man. Not a skeleton hand, white and characteristic, but a black, desiccated hand with yellow joints, with the muscles bare and on them traces of old blood, of blood that seemed like a scale, over the bones sharply cut off at about the middle of the forearm, as with a blow of a hatchet. About the wrist was an enormous iron chain, riveted, soldered to this unclean member, attaching it to the wall by a ring sufficiently strong to hold an elephant.

"I asked: 'What is that?'

"The Englishman responded tranquily:

"'It belonged to my worst enemy. It came from America. It was broken with a saber, cut off with a sharp stone and dried in the sun for eight days. Oh, very good for me, that was!'

"I touched the human relic which must have belonged to a colossus. The fingers were immoderately long and attached by enormous tendons that held the straps of skin in place. This dried hand was frightful to see, making one think, naturally, of the vengeance of a savage.

"I said: 'This man must have been very strong.'

"With gentleness the Englishman answered:

"'Oh yes, but I was stronger than he. I put this chain on him to hold him.'

"I thought he spoke in jest and replied:

"'The chain is useless now that the hand cannot escape.'

"Sir John Rowell replied gravely: 'It always wishes to escape. The chain is necessary.'

"With a rapid, questioning glance I asked myself: 'Is he mad or is that an unpleasant joke?'

"But the face remained impenetrable, tranquil and friendly. I spoke of other things and admired the guns.

"Nevertheless, I noticed three loaded revolvers on the pieces of furniture, as if this man lived in constant fear of attack.

"I went there many times after that; then for some time I did not go. We had become accustomed to his presence; he had become indifferent to us.

"A whole year slipped away. Then one morning toward the end of November my domestic awoke me with the announcement that Sir John Rowell had been assassinated in the night.

"A half-hour later I entered the Englishman's house with the central commissary and the captain of police. The servant, lost in despair, was weeping at the door. I suspected him at first but afterward found that he was innocent.

"The guilty one could never be found.

"Upon entering Sir John's drawing room I perceived his dead body stretched out upon its back in the middle of the room. His waistcoat was torn; a sleeve was hanging, and it was evident that a terrible struggle had taken place.

"The Englishman had been strangled! His frightfully black and swollen face seemed to express an abominable fear; he held something between his set teeth, and his neck, pierced with five holes apparently done with a pointed iron, was covered with blood.

"A doctor joined us. He examined closely the prints of fingers in the flesh and pronounced these strange words:

"'One would think he had been strangled by a skeleton.'

"A shiver ran down my back, and I cast my eyes to the place on the wall where I had seen the horrible, torn-off hand. It was no longer there. The chain was broken and hanging.

"Then I bent over the dead man and found in his mouth a piece of one of the fingers of the missing hand, cut off, or rather sawed off, by the teeth exactly at the second joint.

"Then they tried to collect evidence. They could find nothing. No door had been forced, no window opened or piece of furniture moved. The two watch dogs on the premises had not been aroused.

"Here, in a few words, is the deposition of the servant:

"For a month his master had seemed agitated. He had received many letters which he had burned immediately. Often, taking a whip in anger which seemed like dementia, he had struck in fury this dried hand fastened to the wall and taken, one knew not how, at the moment of a crime.

"He had retired late and shut himself in with care. He always carried arms. Often in the night he talked out loud, as if he were quarreling with someone. On that night, however, there had been no noise, and it was only on coming to open the windows that the servant had found Sir John assassinated. He suspected no one.

"I communicated what I knew of the death to the magistrates and public officers, and they made minute inquiries upon the whole island. They discovered nothing.

"One night, three months after the crime, I had a frightful nightmare. It seemed to me that I saw that hand, that horrible hand, running like a scorpion or a spider along my curtains and my walls. Three times I awoke; three times I fell asleep and again saw that hideous relic galloping about my room, moving its fingers like paws.

"The next day they brought it to me, found in the cemetery upon the tomb where Sir John Rowell was interred—for they had not been able to find his family. The index finger was missing.

"This, ladies, is my story. I know no more about it."

The ladies were terrified, pale and shivering. One of them cried:

"But that is not the end, for there was no explanation! We cannot sleep if you do not tell us what was your idea of the reason of it all."

The magistrate smiled with severity and answered:

"Oh, certainly, ladies, but it will spoil all your terrible dreams. I simply think that the legitimate proprietor of the hand was not dead and that he came for it with the one that remained to him. But I was never able to find out how he did it. It was one kind of revenge."

One of the women murmured:

"No, it could not be thus."

And the judge of information, smiling still, concluded:

"I told you in the beginning that my explanation would not satisfy you."

Ambrose Bierce

The Middle Toe of the Right Foot

I

It is well known that the old Manton house is haunted. In all the rural district near about, and even in the town of Marshall, a mile away, not one person of unbiased mind entertains a doubt of it; incredulity is confined to those opinionated persons who will be called "cranks" as soon as the useful word shall have penetrated the intellectual demesne of the Marshall *Advance.* The evidence that the house is haunted is of two kinds: the testimony of disinterested witnesses who have had ocular proof, and that of the house itself. The former may be disregarded and ruled out on any of the various grounds of objection which may be urged against it by the ingenious; but facts within the observation of all are material and controlling.

In the first place, the Manton house has been unoccupied by mortals for more than ten years, and with its outbuildings is slowly falling into decay—a circumstance which in itself the judicious will hardly venture to ignore. It stands a little way off the loneliest reach of the Marshall and Harriston road, in an opening which was once a farm and is still disfigured with strips of rotting fence and half covered with brambles overrunning a stony and sterile soil long unacquainted with the plow. The house itself is in tolerably good condition, though badly weather-stained and in dire need of attention from the glazier, the smaller male population of the region having attested in the manner of its kind its disapproval of dwelling without dwellers. It is two stories in height, nearly square, its front pierced by a single doorway flanked on each side by a window boarded up to the very top. Corresponding windows above, not protected, serve to admit light and rain to the rooms of the upper floor. Grass and weeds grow pretty rankly all about, and a few shade trees, somewhat the worse for wind, and leaning all in one direction, seem to be making a concerted effort to run away. In short, as the Marshall town humorist explained in the columns of the *Advance*, "the proposition that the Manton house is badly haunted is the only logical conclusion from the premises." The fact that in this dwelling Mr. Manton thought it expedient one night some ten years ago to rise and cut the throats of his wife and two small children, removing at once to another part of the country, has no doubt done its share in directing public attention to the fitness of the place for supernatural phenomena.

To this house, one summer evening, came four men in a wagon. Three of them promptly alighted, and the one who had been driving hitched the team to the only remaining post of what had been a fence. The fourth remained seated in the wagon. "Come," said one of his companions, approaching him, while the others moved away in the direction of the dwelling—"this is the place."

The man addressed did not move. "By God!" he said harshly, "this is a trick, and it looks to me as if you were in it."

"Perhaps I am," the other said, looking him straight in the face and speaking in a tone which had something of contempt in it. "You will remember, however, that the choice of place was with your own assent left to the other side. Of course if you are afraid of spooks—"

"I am afraid of nothing," the man interrupted with another oath, and sprang to the ground. The two then joined the others at the door, which one of them had already opened with some difficulty, caused by rust of lock and hinge. All entered. Inside it was dark, but the man who had unlocked the door produced a candle and matches and made a light. He then unlocked a door on their right as they stood in the passage. This gave them entrance to a large, square room that the candle but dimly lighted. The floor had a thick carpeting of dust, which partly muffled their footfalls. Cobwebs were in the angles of the walls and descended from the ceiling like strips of rotting lace, making undulatory movements in the disturbed air.

The room had two windows in adjoining sides, but from neither could anything be seen except the rough inner surfaces of boards a few inches from the glass. There was no fireplace, no furniture; there was nothing: besides the cobwebs and the dust, the four men were the only objects there which were not a part of the structure.

Strange enough they looked in the yellow light of the candle. The one who had so reluctantly alighted was especially spectacular— he might have been called sensational. He was of middle age, heavily built, deep chested and broad shouldered. Looking at his figure, one would have said that he had a giant's strength; at his features, that he would use it like a giant. He was clean-shaven, his hair rather closely cropped and gray. His low forehead was seamed with wrinkles above the eyes, and over the nose these became vertical. The heavy black brows followed the same law, saved from meeting only by an upward turn at what would otherwise have been the point of contact. Deeply sunken beneath these, glowed in the obscure light a pair of eyes of uncertain color, but obviously enough too small. There was something forbidding in their expression, which was not bettered by the cruel mouth and wide jaw. The nose was well enough, as noses go; one does not expect much of noses. All that was sinister in the man's face seemed accentuated by an unnatural pallor— he appeared altogether bloodless.

The appearance of the other men was sufficiently commonplace: they were such persons as one meets and forgets that he met. All were younger than the man described, between whom and the eldest of the others, who stood apart, there was apparently no kindly feeling. They avoided looking at each other.

"Gentlemen," said the man holding the candle and keys, "I believe everything is right. Are you ready, Mr. Rosser?"

The man standing apart from the group bowed and smiled.

"And you, Mr. Grossmith?"

The heavy man bowed and scowled.

"You will be pleased to remove your outer clothing."

Their hats, coats, waistcoats and neckwear were soon removed and thrown outside the door, in the passage. The man with the candle now nodded, and the fourth man—he who had urged Grossmith to leave the wagon—produced from the pocket of his overcoat two long, murderous-looking bowie knives, which he drew now from their leather scabbards.

"They are exactly alike," he said, presenting one to each of the two principals—for by this time the dullest observer would have understood the nature of this meeting. It was to be a duel to the death.

Each combatant took a knife, examined it critically near the candle and tested the strength of blade and handle across his lifted knee. Their persons were then searched in turn, each by the second of the other.

"If it is agreeable to you, Mr. Grossmith," said the man holding the light, "you will place yourself in that corner."

He indicated the angle of the room farthest from the door, whither Grossmith retired, his second parting from him with a grasp of the hand which had nothing of cordiality in it. In the angle nearest the door Mr. Rosser stationed himself, and after a whispered consultation his second left him, joining the other near the door. At that moment the candle was suddenly extinguished, leaving all in profound darkness. This may have been done by a draft from the opened door; whatever the cause, the effect was startling.

"Gentlemen," said a voice which sounded strangely unfamiliar in the altered condition affecting the relations of the senses—"gentlemen, you will not move until you hear the closing of the outer door."

A sound of trampling ensued, then the closing of the inner door; and finally the outer one closed with a concussion which shook the entire building.

A few minutes afterward a belated farmer's boy met a light wagon which was being driven furiously toward the town of Marshall. He declared that behind the two figures on the front seat stood a third, with its hands upon the bowed shoulders of the others, who appeared to struggle vainly to free themselves from its grasp. This figure, unlike the others, was clad in white, and had undoubtedly boarded the wagon as it passed the haunted house. As the lad could boast a considerable former experience with the supernatural thereabouts his word had the weight justly due to the testimony of an expert.

The story (in connection with the next day's events) eventually appeared in the *Advance,* with some slight literary embellishments and a concluding intimation that the gentlemen referred to would be allowed the use of the paper's columns for their version of the night's adventure. But the privilege remained without a claimant.

II

The events that led up to this "duel in the dark" were simple enough. One evening three young men of the town of Marshall were sitting in a quiet corner of the porch of the village hotel, smoking and discussing such matters as three educated young men of a Southern village would naturally find interesting. Their names were King, Sancher, and Rosser. At a little distance, within easy hearing, but taking no part in the conversation, sat a fourth. He was a stranger to the others. They merely knew that on his arrival by the stagecoach that afternoon he had written in the hotel register the name Robert Grossmith. He had not been observed to speak to anyone except the hotel clerk. He seemed, indeed, singularly fond of his own company—or, as the *personnel* of the *Advance* expressed it, "grossly addicted to evil associations." But then it should be said in justice to the stranger that the *personnel* was himself of a too convivial disposition fairly to judge one differently gifted, and had, moreover, experienced a slight rebuff in an effort at an "interview."

"I hate any kind of deformity in a woman," said King, "whether natural or—acquired. I have a theory that any physical defect has its correlative mental and moral defect."

"I infer, then," said Rosser, gravely, "that a lady lacking the moral advantage of a nose would find the struggle to become Mrs. King an arduous enterprise."

"Of course you may put it that way," was the reply; "but, seriously, I once threw over a most charming girl on learning quite accidentally that she had suffered amputation of a toe. My conduct was brutal if you like, but if I had married that girl I should have been miserable for life and should have made her so."

"Whereas," said Sancher, with a light laugh, "by marrying a gentleman of more liberal views she escaped with a parted throat."

"Ah, you know to whom I refer. Yes, she married Manton, but I don't know about his liberality; I'm not sure but he cut her throat because he discovered that she lacked that excellent thing in woman, the middle toe of the right foot."

"Look at that chap!" said Rosser in a low voice, his eyes fixed upon the stranger.

That chap was obviously listening intently to the conversation.

"Damn his impudence!" muttered King—"what ought we to do?"

"That's an easy one," Rosser replied, rising. "Sir," he continued, addressing the stranger, "I think it would be better if you would remove your chair to the other end of the veranda. The presence of gentlemen is evidently an unfamiliar situation to you."

The man sprang to his feet and strode forward with clenched hands, his face white with rage. All were now standing. Sancher stepped between the belligerents.

"You are hasty and unjust," he said to Rosser; "this gentleman has done nothing to deserve such language."

But Rosser would not withdraw a word. By the custom of the country and the time there could be but one outcome to the quarrel.

"I demand the satisfaction due to a gentleman," said the stranger, who had become more calm. "I have not an acquaintance in this region. Perhaps you, sir," bowing to Sancher, "will be kind enough to represent me in this matter."

Sancher accepted the trust—somewhat reluctantly it must be confessed, for the man's appearance and manner were not at all to his liking. King, who during the colloquy had hardly removed his eyes from the stranger's face and had not spoken a word, consented with a nod to act for Rosser, and the upshot of it was that, the principals having retired, a meeting was arranged for the next evening. The nature of the arrangements has been already disclosed. The duel with knives in a dark room was once a commoner feature of Southwestern life than it is likely to be again. How thin a veneering of "chivalry" covered the essential brutality of the code under which such encounters were possible we shall see.

III

In the blaze of a midsummer noonday the old Manton house was hardly true to its traditions. It was of the earth, earthy. The sunshine caressed it warmly and affectionately, with evident disregard of its bad reputation. The grass greening all the expanse in its front seemed to grow, not rankly, but with a natural and joyous exuberance, and the weeds blossomed quite like plants. Full of charming lights and shadows and populous with pleasant-voiced birds, the neglected shade trees no longer struggled to run away, but bent reverently beneath their burdens of sun and song. Even in the glassless upper windows were an expression of peace and contentment, due to the light within. Over the stony fields the visible heat danced with a lively tremor incompatible with the gravity which is an attribute of the supernatural.

Such was the aspect under which the place presented itself to Sheriff Adams and two other men who had come out from Marshall to look at it. One of these men was Mr. King, the sheriff's deputy; the other, whose name was Brewer, was a brother of the late Mrs. Manton. Under a beneficent law of the State relating to property which has been for a certain period abandoned by an owner whose residence cannot be ascertained, the sheriff was legal custodian of the Manton farm and appurtenances thereunto belonging. His present visit was in mere perfunctory compliance with some order of a court in which

Mr. Brewer had an action to get possession of the property as heir to his desceased sister. By a mere coincidence, the visit was made on the day after the night that Deputy King had unlocked the house for another and very different purpose. His presence now was not of his own choosing: he had been ordered to accompany his superior and at the moment could think of nothing more prudent than simulated alacrity in obedience to the command.

Carelessly opening the front door, which to his surprise was not locked, the sheriff was amazed to see, lying on the floor of the passage in which it opened, a confused heap of men's apparel. Examination showed it to consist of two hats, and the same number of coats, waistcoats, and scarves, all in a remarkably good state of preservation, albeit somewhat defiled by the dust in which they lay. Mr. Brewer was equally astonished, but Mr. King's emotion is not of record. With a new and lively interest in his own actions the sheriff now unlatched and pushed open a door on the right, and the three entered. The room was apparently vacant—no; as their eyes became accustomed to the dimmer light something was visible in the farthest angle of the wall. It was a human figure—that of a man crouching close in the corner. Something in the attitude made the intruders halt when they had barely passed the threshold. The figure more and more clearly defined itself. The man was upon one knee, his back in the angle of the wall, his shoulders elevated to the level of his ears, his hands before his face, palms outward, the fingers spread and crooked like claws; the white face turned upward on the retracted neck had an expression of unutterable fright, the mouth half-open, the eyes incredibly expanded. He was stone dead. Yet, with the exception of a bowie knife, which had evidently fallen from his own hand, not another object was in the room.

In thick dust that covered the floor were some confused footprints near the door and along the wall through which it opened. Along one of the adjoining walls, too, past the boarded-up windows, was the trail made by the man himself in reaching his corner. Instinctively in approaching the body the three men followed that trail. The sheriff grasped one of the outthrown arms; it was as rigid as iron, and the application of a gentle force rocked the entire body without altering the relation of its parts. Brewer, pale with excitement, gazed intently into the distorted face. "God of mercy!" he suddenly cried, "it is Manton!"

"You are right," said King, with an evident attempt at calmness: "I knew Manton. He then wore a full beard and his hair long, but this is he."

He might have added: "I recognized him when he challenged Rosser. I told Rosser and Sancher who he was before we played him this horrible trick. When Rosser left this dark room at our heels, forgetting his outer clothing in the excitement, and driving away with us in his shirt sleeves—all through the discreditable proceedings we knew whom we were dealing with, murderer and coward that he was!"

But nothing of this did Mr. King say. With his better light he was trying to penetrate the mystery of the man's death. That he had not once moved from the corner where he had been stationed; that his posture was that of neither attack nor defense; that he had dropped his weapon; that he had obviously perished of sheer horror of something that he *saw*—these were circumstances which Mr. King's disturbed intelligence could not rightly comprehend.

Groping in intellectual darkness for a clue to his maze of doubt, his gaze, directed mechanically downward in the way of one who ponders momentous matters, fell upon something which, there, in the light of day and in the presence of living companions, affected him with terror. In the dust of years that lay thick upon the floor—leading from the door by which they had entered, straight across the room to within a yard of Manton's crouching corpse—were three parallel lines of footprints—light but definite impressions of bare feet, the outer ones those of small children, the inner a woman's. From the point at which they ended they did not return; they pointed all one way. Brewer, who had observed them at the same moment, was leaning forward in an attitude of rapt attention, horribly pale.

"Look at that!" he cried, pointing with both hands at the nearest print of the woman's right foot, where she had apparently stopped and stood. "The middle toe is missing—it was Gertrude!"

Gertrude was the late Mrs. Manton, sister to Mr. Brewer.

J.S. LeFanu

Dickon the Devil

About thirty years ago I was selected by two rich old maids to visit a property in that part of Lancashire which lies near the famous forest of Pendle, with which Mr. Ainsworth's "Lancashire Witches" has made us so pleasantly familiar. My business was to make partition of a small property including a house and demesne, to which they had a long time before succeeded as co-heiresses.

The last forty miles of my journey I was obliged to post, chiefly by crossroads, little known, and less frequented, and presenting scenery often extremely interesting and pretty. The picturesqueness of the landscape was enhanced by the season, the beginning of September, at which I was traveling.

I had never been in this part of the world before; I am told it is now a great deal less wild, and, consequently, less beautiful.

At the inn where I had stopped for a relay of horses and some dinner—for it was then past five o'clock—I found the host, a hale old fellow of five-and-sixty, as he told me, a man of easy and garrulous benevolence, willing to accommodate his guests with any amount of talk, which the slightest tap sufficed to set flowing, on any subject you pleased.

I was curious to learn something about Barwyke, which was the name of the demesne and house I was going to. As there was no inn within some miles of it, I had written to the steward to put me up there, the best way he could, for a night.

The host of the "Three Nuns," which was the sign under which he entertained wayfarers, had not a great deal to tell. It was twenty years, or more, since old Squire Bowes died, and no one had lived in the Hall ever since, except the gardener and his wife.

"Tom Wyndsour will be as old a man as myself; but he's a bit taller, and not so much in flesh, quite," said the fat innkeeper.

"But there were stories about the house," I repeated, "that they said, prevented tenants from coming into it?"

"Old wives' tales; many years ago, that will be, sir; I forget 'em; I forget 'em all. Oh yes, there always will be, when a house is left so; foolish folk will always be talkin'; but I hadn't heard a word about it this twenty year."

It was vain trying to pump him; the old landlord of the "Three Nuns," for some reason, did not choose to tell tales of Barwyke Hall, if he really did, as I suspected, remember them.

I paid my reckoning, and resumed my journey, well pleased with the good cheer of that old-world inn, but a little disappointed.

We had been driving for more than an hour, when we began to cross a wild common; and I knew that, this passed, a quarter of an hour would bring me to the door of Barwyke Hall.

The peat and furze were pretty soon left behind; we were again in the wooded scenery that I enjoyed so much, so entirely natural and pretty, and so little disturbed by traffic of any kind. I was looking from the chaise window, and soon detected the object of which, for some time, my eye had been in search. Barwyke Hall was a large, quaint house, of that cage-work fashion known as "black-and-white," in which the bars and angles of an oak framework contrast, black as ebony, with the white plaster that overspreads the masonry built into its interstices. This steep-roofed Elizabethan house stood in the midst of park-like grounds of no great extent, but rendered imposing by the noble stature of the old trees that now cast their lengthening shadows eastward over the sward, from the declining sun.

The park wall was gray with age, and in many places laden with ivy. In deep gray shadow, that contrasted with the dim fires of evening reflected on the foliage above it, in a gentle hollow, stretched a lake that looked cold and black, and seemed, as it were, to skulk from observation with a guilty knowledge.

I had forgot that there was a lake at Barwyke; but the moment this caught my eye, like the cold polish of a snake in the shadow, my instinct seemed to recognize something dangerous, and I knew that the lake was connected, I could not remember how, with the story I had heard of this place in my boyhood.

I drove up a grass-grown avenue, under the boughs of these noble trees, whose foliage, dyed in autumnal red and yellow, returned the beams of the western sun gorgeously.

We drew up at the door. I got out, and had a good look at the front of the house; it was a large and melancholy mansion, with signs of long neglect upon it; great wooden shutters, in the old fashion, were barred, outside, across the windows; grass, and even nettles, were growing thick on the courtyard, and a thin moss streaked the timber beams; the plaster was discolored by time and weather, and bore great russet and yellow stains. The gloom was increased by several grand old trees that crowded close about the house.

I mounted the steps, and looked round; the dark lake lay near me now, a little to the left. It was not large; it may have covered some ten or twelve acres; but it added to the melancholy of the scene. Near the center of it was a small island, with two old ash trees, leaning toward each other, their pensive images reflected in the stirless water. The only cheery influence in this scene of antiquity, solitude, and neglect was that the house and landscape were warmed with the ruddy western beams. I knocked, and my summons resounded hollow and ungenial in my ear; and the bell, from far away, returned a deep-mouthed and surly ring, as if it resented being roused from a score years' slumber.

A light-limbed, jolly-looking old fellow, in a barracan jacket and gaiters, with a smile of welcome, and a very sharp, red nose, that seemed to promise good cheer, opened the door with a promptitude that indicated a hospitable expectation of my arrival.

There was but little light in the hall, and that little lost itself in darkness in the background. It was very spacious and lofty, with a gallery running round it, which, when the door was open, was visible at two or three points. Almost in the dark my new acquaintance led me across this wide hall into the room destined for my reception. It was spacious, and wainscoted up to the ceiling. The furniture of this capacious chamber was old-fashioned and clumsy. There were curtains still to the windows, and a piece of Turkish carpet lay upon the floor; those windows were two in number, looking out, through the trunks of the trees close to the house, upon the lake. It needed all the fire, and all the pleasant associations of my entertainer's red nose, to light up this melancholy chamber. A door at its farther end admitted to the room that was prepared for my sleeping apartment. It was wainscoted, like the other. It had a four-post bed, with heavy tapestry cutains, and in other respects was furnished in the same old-world and ponderous style as the other room. Its window, like those of that apartment, looked out upon the lake.

Somber and sad as these rooms were, they were yet scrupulously clean. I had nothing to complain of; but the effect was rather dispiriting.

Having given some directions about supper—a pleasant incident to look forward to—and made a rapid toilet, I called on my friend with the gaiters and red nose (Tom Wyndsour) whose occupation was that of a "bailiff," or under-steward, of the property, to accompany me, as we had still an hour or so of sun and twilight, in a walk over the grounds.

It was a sweet autumn evening, and my guide, a hardy old fellow, strode at a pace that tasked me to keep up with.

Among clumps of trees at the northern boundary of the demesne we lighted upon the little antique parish church. I was looking down upon it, from an eminence, and the park wall interposed; but a little way down was a stile affording access to the road, and by this we approached the iron gate of the churchyard. I saw the church door open; the sexton was replacing his pick, shovel, and spade, with which he had just been digging a grave in the churchyard, in their little repository under the stone stair of the tower. He was a polite, shrewd little hunchback, who was very happy to show me over the church. Among the monuments was one that interested me; it was erected to commemorate the very Squire Bowes from whom my two old maids had inherited the house and estate of Barwyke. It spoke of him in terms of grandiloquent eulogy, and informed the Christian reader that he had died, in the bosom of the Church of England, at the age of seventy-one.

I read this inscription by the parting beams of the setting sun, which disappeared behind the horizon just as we passed out from under the porch.

"Twenty years since the Squire died," said I, reflecting as I loitered still in the churchyard.

"Ay, sir; 'twill be twenty year the ninth o' last month."

"And a very good old gentleman?"

"Good-natured enough, and an easy gentleman he was, sir; I don't think while he lived he ever hurt a fly," acquiesced Tom Wyndsour. "It ain't always easy sayin' what's in 'em though, and what they may take or turn to afterwards; and some o' them sort, I think, goes mad."

"You don't think he was out of his mind?" I asked.

"He? La! no; not he, sir; a bit lazy, mayhap, like other old fellows; but a knew devilish well what he was about."

Tom Wyndsour's account was a little enigmatical; but, like old Squire Bowes, I was "a bit lazy" that evening, and asked no more questions about him.

We got over the stile upon the narrow road that skirts the churchyard. It is overhung by elms more than a hundred years old, and in the twilight, which now prevailed, was growing very dark. As side-by-side we walked along this road, hemmed in by two loose stone-like walls, something running towards us in a ziz-zag line passed us at a wild pace, with a sound like a frightened laugh or a shudder, and I saw, as it passed, that it was a human figure. I may confess now, that I was a little startled. The dress of this figure was, in part, white: I know I mistook it at first for a white horse coming down the road at a gallop. Tom Wyndsour turned about and looked after the retreating figure.

"He'll be on his travels tonight," he said, in a low tone. "Easy served with a bed, *that* lad be; six foot o' dry peat or heath, or a nook in a dry ditch. That lad hasn't slept once in a house this twenty year, and never will while grass grows."

"Is he mad?" I asked.

"Something that way, sir; he's an idiot, an awpy; we call him 'Dickon the devil,' because the devil's almost the only word that's ever in his mouth."

It struck me that this idiot was in some way connected with the story of old Squire Bowes.

"Queer things are told of him, I dare say?" I suggested.

"More or less, sir; more or less. Queer stories, some."

"Twenty years since he slept in a house? That's about the time the Squire died," I continued.

"So it will be, sir; and not very long after."

"You must tell me all about that, Tom, tonight, when I can hear it comfortably, after supper."

Tom did not seem to like my invitation; and looking straight before him as we trudged on, he said,

"You see, sir, the house has been quiet, and the nout's been troubling folk inside the walls or out, all round the woods of Barwyke, this ten year, or more; and my old woman, down there, is clear against talking about such matters, and thinks it best—and so do I—to let sleepin' dogs be."

He dropped his voice towards the close of the sentence, and nodded significantly.

We soon reached a point where he unlocked a wicket in the park wall, by which we entered the grounds of Barwyke once more.

The twilight deepening over the landscape, the huge and solemn trees, and the distant outline of the haunted house, exercised a somber influence on me, which, together with the fatigue of a day of travel, and the brisk walk we had had, disinclined me to interrupt the silence in which my companion now indulged.

A certain air of comparative comfort, on our arrival, in great measure dissipated the gloom that was stealing over me. Although it was by no means a cold night, I was very glad to see some wood blazing in the grate; and a pair of candles aiding the light of the fire, made the room look cheerful. A small table, with a very white cloth, and preparations for supper, was also a very agreeable object.

I should have liked very well, under these influences, to have listened to Tom Wyndsour's story; but after supper I grew too sleepy to attempt to lead him to the subject; and after yawning for a time, I found there was no use in contending against my drowsiness, so I betook myself to my bedroom, and by ten o'clock was fast asleep.

What interruption I experienced that night I shall tell you presently. It was not much but it was very odd.

By next night I had completed my work at Barwyke. From early morning till then I was so incessantly occupied and hard-worked, that I had not time to think over the singular occurrence to which I have just referred. Behold me, however, at length once more seated at my little supper table, having ended a comfortable meal. It had been a sultry day, and I had thrown one of the large windows up as high as it would go. I was sitting near it, with my brandy and water at my elbow, looking out into the dark. There was no moon, and the trees that are grouped about the house make the darkness round it supernaturally profound on such nights.

"Tom," said I, so soon as the jug of hot punch I had supplied him with began to exercise its genial and communicative influence; "you must tell me who beside your wife and you and myself slept in the house last night."

Tom, sitting near the door, set down his tumbler, and looked at me askance, while you might count seven, without speaking a word.

"Who else slept in the house?" he repeated, very deliberately. "Not a living soul, sir"; and he looked hard at me, still evidently expecting something more.

"That *is* very odd," I said returning his stare, and feeling really a little odd. "You are sure *you* were not in my room last night?"

"Not till I came to call you, sir, this morning; *I* can make oath of that."

"Well," said I, "there was some one there, *I* can make oath of that. I was so tired I could not make up my mind to get up; but I was waked by a sound that I thought as someone flinging down the two tin boxes in which my papers were locked up violently on the floor. I heard a slow step on the ground, and there was light in the room, although I remembered having put out my candle. I thought it must have been you, who had come in for my clothes, and upset the boxes by accident. Whoever it was, he went out and the light with him. I was about to settle again, when, the curtain being a little open at the foot of the bed, I saw a light on the wall opposite; such as a candle from outside would cast if the door were very cautiously opening. I started up in the bed, drew the side curtain, and saw that the door *was* opening, and admitting light from outside. It is close, you know, to the head of the bed. A hand was holding on the edge of the door and pushing it open; not a bit like yours; a very singular hand. Let me look at yours."

He extended it for my inspection.

"Oh no; there's nothing wrong with your hand. This was differently shaped; fatter; and the middle finger was stunted, and shorter than the rest, looking as if it had once been broken, and the nail was crooked like a claw. I called out 'Who's there?' and the light and the hand were withdrawn, and I saw and heard no more of my visitor."

"So sure as you're a living man, that was him!" exclaimed Tom Wyndsour, his very nose growing pale, and his eyes almost starting out of his head.

"Who?" I asked.

"Old Squire Bowes; 'twas *his* hand you saw; the Lord a' mercy on us!" answered Tom. "The broken finger, and the nail bent like a hoop. Well for you, sir, he didn't come back when you called, that time. You came here about them Miss Dymock's business, and he never meant they should have a foot o' ground in Barwyke; and he was making a will to give it away quite different, when death took him short. He never was uncivil to no one; but he couldn't abide them ladies. My mind misgave me when I heard 'twas about their business you were coming; and now you see how it is; he'll be at his old tricks again!"

With some pressure and a little more punch, I induced Tom Wyndsour to explain his mysterious allusions by recounting the occurrences which followed the old Squire's death.

"Squire Bowes of Barwyke died without making a will, as you know," said Tom. "And all the folk round were sorry; that is to say, sir, as sorry as folk will be for an old man that has seen a long tale of years, and has no right to grumble that death has knocked an hour too soon at his door. The Squire was well liked; he was never in a passion, or said a hard word; and he would not hurt a fly; and that made what happened after his decease the more surprising.

"The first thing these ladies did, when they got the property, was to buy stock for the park.

"It was not wise, in any case, to graze the land on their own account. But they little new all they had to contend with.

"Before long something went wrong with the cattle; first one, and then another, took sick and died, and so on, till the loss began to grow heavy. Then, queer stories, little by little, began to be told. It was said, first by one, then by another, that Squire Bowes was seen, about evening time, walking, just as he used to do when he was alive, among the old trees, leaning on his stick; and, sometimes when he came up with the cattle, he would stop and lay his hand kindly like on the back of one of them; and that one was sure to fall sick next day, and die soon after.

"No one ever met him in the park, or in the woods, or ever saw him, except a good distance off. But they knew his gait and his figure well, and the clothes he used to wear; and they could tell the beast he laid his hand on by its color—white, dun, or black; and that beast was sure to sicken and die. The neighbors grew shy of taking the path over the park; and no one liked to walk in the woods, or come inside the bounds of Barwyke: and the cattle went on sickening and dying as before.

"At that time there was one Thomas Pyke; he had been a groom to the old Squire; and he was in care of the place, and was the only one that used to sleep in the house.

"Tom was vexed, hearing these stories; which he did not believe the half on 'em; and more especial as he could not get man or boy to herd the cattle; all being afeared. So he wrote to Matlock in Derbyshire, for his brother, Richard Pyke, a clever lad, and one that knew nout o' the story of the old Squire walking.

"Dick came; and the cattle was better; folk said they could still see the old Squire, sometimes, walking, as before, in openings of the wood, with his stick in his hand; but he was shy of coming nigh the cattle, whatever his reason might be, since Dickon Pyke came; and he used to stand a long bit off, looking at them, with no more stir in him than a trunk o' one of the old trees, for an hour at a time, till the shape melted away, little by little, like the smoke of a fire that burns out.

"Tom Pyke and his brother Dickon, being the only living souls in the house, lay in the big bed in the servants' room, the house being fast barred and locked, one night in November.

"Tom was lying next the wall, and he told me, as wide-awake as ever he was at noonday. His brother Dickon lay outside, and was sound asleep.

"Well, as Tom lay thinking, with his eyes turned toward the door, it opens slowly, and who should come in but old Squire Bowes, his face lookin' as dead as he was in his coffin.

"Tom's very breath left his body; he could not take his eyes off him; and he felt the hair rising up on his head.

"The Squire came to the side of the bed, and put his arms under Dickon, and lifted the boy—in a dead sleep all the time—and carried him out so, at the door.

"Such was the appearance, to Tom Pyke's eyes, and he was ready to swear to it, anywhere.

"When this happened, the light, wherever it came from, all on a sudden went out, and Tom could not see his own hand before him.

"More dead than alive, he lay till daylight.

"Sure enough his brother Dickon was gone. No sign of him could he discover about the house; and with some trouble he got a couple of the neighbors to help him to search the woods and grounds. Not a sign of him anywhere.

"At last one of them thought of the island in the lake; the little boat was moored to the old post at the water's edge. In they got, though with small